D1625043

2-15

Written by Jenny Bornholdt

Illustrated by Sarah Wilkins

A Book
is a
Book

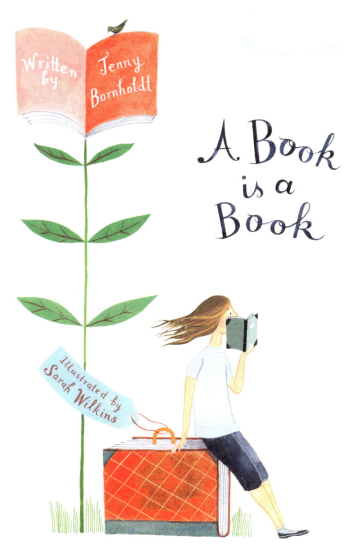

GECKO PRESS

WHITIREIA PUBLISHING

First published in 2013 by
Gecko Press and Whitireia Publishing

Gecko Press | PO Box 9335,
Marion Square, Wellington 6141
New Zealand
info@geckopress.com

Whitireia New Zealand | Private Bag 50910,
Porirua City 5240

Distributed in New Zealand by Random House NZ
Distributed in Australia by Scholastic Australia
Distributed in the United Kingdom by Bounce Sales & Marketing
Distributed in the United States by Lerner Publishing Group

Text © Jenny Bornholdt 2013
Illustrations © Sarah Wilkins 2013

A catalogue record for this book is available from the
National Library of New Zealand.

Gecko Press acknowledges the generous support of Creative New Zealand.

Designed by Vida & Luke Kelly, New Zealand
Printed in China by Everbest Printing Co Ltd,
an accredited ISO 14001 & FSC certified printer

ISBN hardback: 978-1-877579-92-9

For more curiously good books, visit www.geckopress.com

This book celebrates the 20th birthday of the Whitireia
publishing programme. We developed the idea through
much conversation with publishers, writers, and editors—
many of whom are our graduates—and of course Gecko
Press: a collaboration that reflects our bond with the
publishing industry. At our heart is making
books for readers, and we trust this
book is a fitting celebration of that.
Find out more about the story of
A Book is a Book and our editing
and publishing training at
www.whitireiapublishing.co.nz

All thanks to
Carlo Gamble,
Emily Lawson,
Ivy and Paul Austin
for their thoughts
about books.

Carlo proved to be an
expert on many things,
including why some books
are shorter than others
and the connection between
the written word
and volcanoes.
Thanks Carlo.

A book is to read.

A book is paper and small or big.
You can read the words in it
and you can do this heaps of times.

Books can be true and not true
and sometimes they can be
both at the same time.

A book belongs in a library,
on a bookshelf, in a bookshop,
in your house.

A story belongs wherever a story belongs.

Reading a book of pictures is still reading.

Sometimes babies chew books.

Sometimes dogs do too,
but not usually.

If it's Sunday and raining,
a book is the perfect thing.
Even a small book, because
boredom can be very big.

You can go right inside a book.

Reading books in bed is great,
but not really heavy ones.

You will find books about
cattle rustling, and everything
else that's useful, at the library.

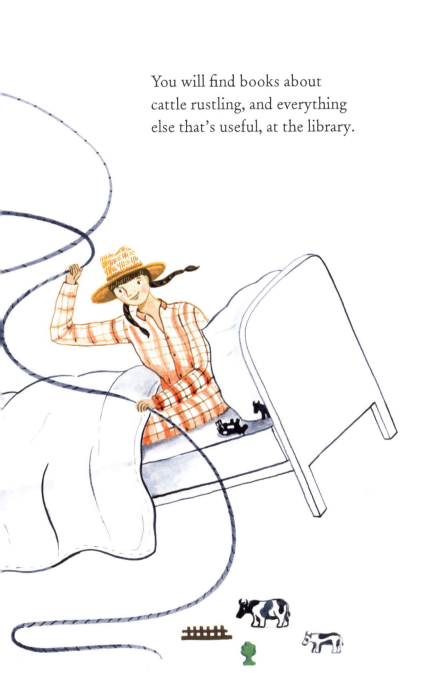

If you want a horse, you can read
a book about horses and then you
don't have to get one yourself.
Horses need a lot of grass and you
have to wear a weird hat.

If you don't have a book
you should get yourself a dog.

Scary is good.

If you read late at night, deep down in your bed, you will wish you had a glow-in-the-dark book because that would make secret reading easy as pie.

Whatever that means.

Some books are small because
some writers are very tired.

You can read a book while you
walk, but you have to be careful
not to bump into things.

You can read in the bath but you mustn't drop your book.

It is impossible to read in the shower.

It can be really good to read a book in a tree.

Books are good for covering
up accidents with jam.

If you really don't like a book
you can put it in the compost.

How a book smells depends
on what it's been through.
If it has been accidentally
dropped in soup then it
will smell like soup.

A book smells
kind of dry, like
cauliflower.

If your guinea pig
sits on it, it will
smell like that.

Sometimes you lose your place in a book
and sometimes someone like your aunt
will give you a bookmark with trees of
the world on it, but then you lose that too.

Books can be on top of each other
or beside each other like this: book
book book book book book book.

If you need to get around your room
without touching the floor, books are good.
You should only use your biggest, worst
books for this game.

A book is a door because
it opens into a house.

A house is like a book
because it has a door.

Magicians can make things
come out of books. Sometimes
money, but never jelly.

A book can never run out of power.

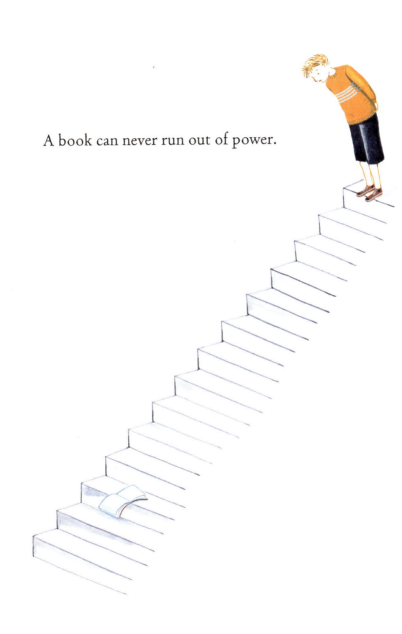

Except, of course, if it gets ripped
and thrown in lava.

If you love a book you can lend it to your friend and they might lend it to another friend and then they might lend it to a different friend and it can go on like that to infinity.

A book is a book.